MONSTER, MONSTER, UNDER MY BED

Sandra Campagna-Clark

Charleston, SC

First Edition

Paperback ISBN: 9781649906786
Hardcover ISBN: 9781649906793

For Lilah, my brave girl with the big heart. Mommy will always be by your side to chase your monsters away.

Monster, Monster,
under my bed.
Monster, Monster, is
it in my head?

Monster, Monster, are you staring at me?

OMG! I count...

3
Three!

1
One..

2 Two...

That Monster, Monster, under my bed has... three great, big, giant, fleas.

What's that I hear?

I can't catch a wink because that smooshy faced monster is a great, big, ball of stink!

Instead, I pinch my nose
and whisper scream
for my sister Belle.

Belle

It's bedtime I do know,
so under the covers I will go...

but I must take one look below.

My fear will not show,

and I take a peek very...very...slow.

What googly eyed, smooshy faced,
hungry, snuffling ball of stink,
Monster, Monster, can this be?

With my official, unofficial degree in Monsterology...

BRAVERY UNIVERSITY
has awarded

Lilah Clark

Diploma for the Official, Unofficial Degree

Master of the Boogie Monster in Monsterology

dr. frank einstein
Dean of the Littles

Courage

I put on my
courage cape
with great curiosity,

and...what-whattt??
I do declare that Monster, Monster,
has a great, big, wiggly butt!

There, the Monster, Monster,
finally sat.

Can it be??

It's Henri!!

Nighty, night, Henri.

The End

me & henri

CPSIA information can be obtained
at www.ICGtesting.com
Printed in the USA
LVHW072047160321
681673LV00026B/1348